P9-CAN-548

RACHEL ISADORA

Friends

Greenwillow Books, New York

Visiting

Building

Drawing

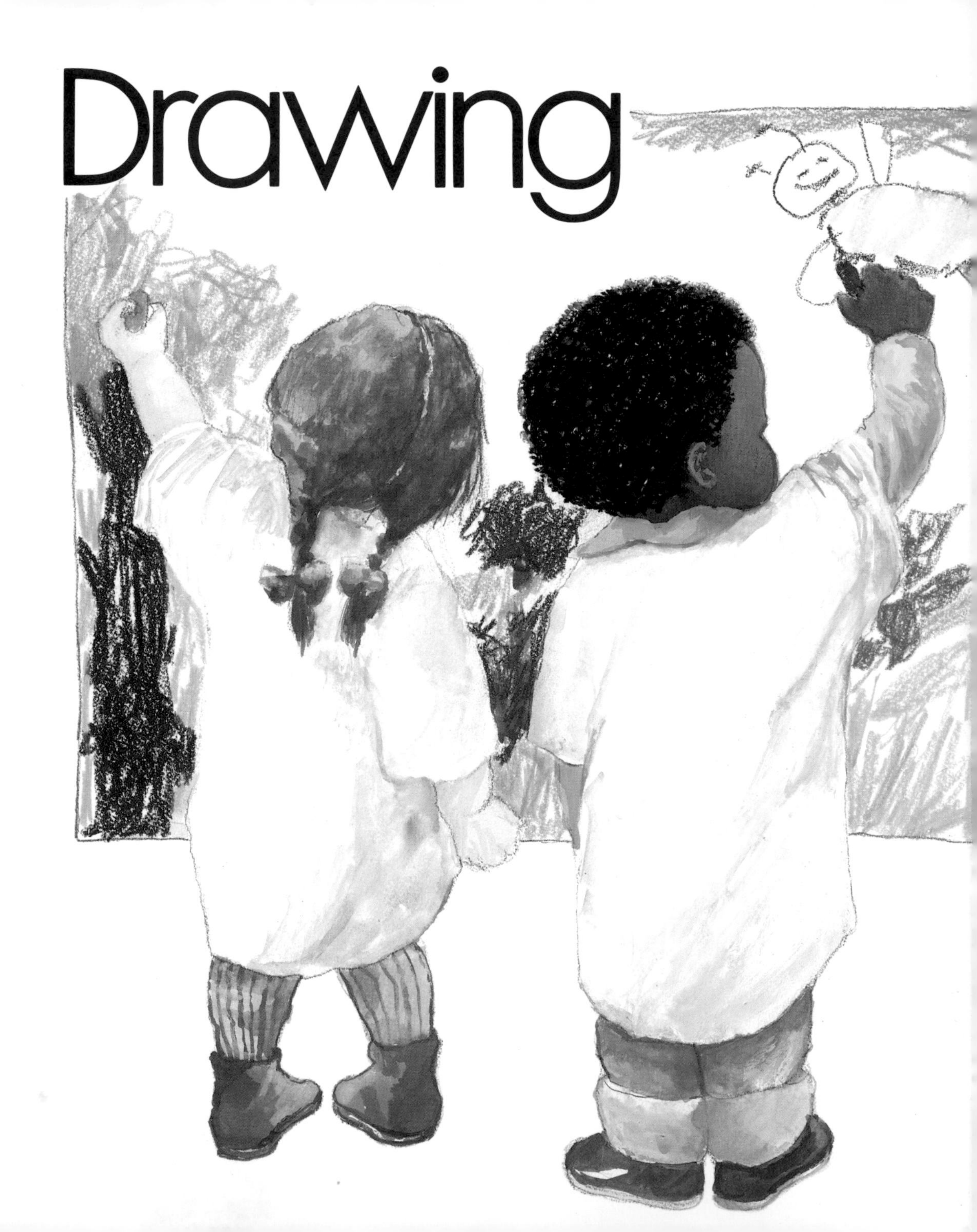

Laughing

Jumping

Playing

Reading

Smelling

Sharing

Hugging

Waving good-bye

Watercolor paints were used for the full-color art. The text type is Futura Book.

Printed in Hong Kong by South China Printing Company (1988) Ltd.
First Edition 10 9 8 7 6 5 4 3 2 1

FOR NICHOLAS JAMES MAXIMILLIAN

Library of Congress Cataloging-in-Publication Data
Isadora, Rachel.
Friends / Rachel Isadora.
p. cm.
Summary: Labeled pictures portray children visiting, building, drawing, laughing, hugging, and engaging in similar friendly pursuits.
ISBN 0-688-08264-5. ISBN 0-688-08265-3 (lib. bdg.)
[1. Friendship—Fiction.] I. Title.
PZ7.I763Fr 1990
[E]—dc19
89-11753 CIP AC